THE SPELLMASTER'S BOOK

BOOK ONE IN THE LEGENDS OF MYTHERIOS

JAMES KEITH

JAMES KEITH
AUTHOR

The Spellmaster's Book
Legends of Mytherios - Book One

Copyright © 2020 James Keith
All rights reserved.

This book is a work of fiction. Names, characters, places and incidents are products of the author's imagination or are used fictitiously. Any resemblance to actual events, locales, or persons living or dead, is entirely coincidental.

Editing Services Provided by Dark Raven Edits
www.facebook.com/darkraveneedits

Cover Created by Phycel Designs
www.phycel.com

SYNOPSIS

Hidden deep within the sewers of our world roosts a vile creature known only as The Dark Goblin. He holds in his possession The Spellmaster's Book, a text with the power to make him practically immortal. He fears no one, and turns all those who dare cross him into brainless goblins who obey his every command.

Siblings Andy and Josie have heard rumors of The Dark Goblin and begin to fear he may be behind the mysterious disappearance of their father. Together, they embark on a quest to reclaim the legendary Spellmaster's Book and free all of those who have been cursed by the malevolent goblin.

As darkness closes in on Andy and Josie from all sides, they discover the greatest weapon they have to wield has been inside them all along.

For Leah-Jane my beautiful daughter with her vivid imagination who has helped me bring these characters to life.

DEEP DOWN IN THE DARK DAMP SEWERS, THERE is a legend, a legend of the Goblin army. Which are led by none other, than The Dark Goblin. Legend has it that The Dark Goblin carries with him a book. This is no ordinary book. This book is the Spellmaster's book. It was taken by a Goblin many centuries ago. It has unique powers and can cast some of the most powerful magical spells the world has ever seen. With the book comes a curse, when anyone who tries to steal the book from The Dark Goblin, becomes a Goblin themselves. Over the years many people have gone missing in the sewers, the legend has it is that they tried to steal the Spellmaster's book but became Goblins instead. Legend speaks of a boy, with the power to repel the spell. This boy will break the curse of the Goblins and free them all back into their human form. The Goblins worship The Dark Goblin, they are in awe of his powers. The ability he has to cast any spell that he wishes.

"Andy, what an amazing story," said Josie in a very excitable voice.

"This is no story, this is a legend and together we are going to find the Spellmaster's book and break the curse of The Dark Goblin," sniggered Andy with a huge smile on his face. Andy loved the story of The Dark Goblin and all the Goblins that lived in the sewers. It was his dream to head down to the sewers to face The Dark Goblin, claim the Spellmaster's book and break the curse of the Goblins to free them all from their evil. Andy closed his storybook and stood at his window. "Josie, come here," he called. Josie stood up and walked to the window.

"What are we looking at Andy?" she asked. Andy pointed across his garden to the main road.

"See that manhole cover," he said.

"Yes, what about it?" asked Josie.

"That is where we make our entrance to the sewers," he laughed. Josie gulped, she was claustrophobic and hated small spaces.

"I can't go down there," she cried.

"Of, course you can, it will be an amazing

adventure for both of us," replied Andy. Josie was not convinced, the idea of being in the dark, dirty, smelly sewer was not her idea of an adventure, it scared her to death.

"Dinner is ready," came a voice from downstairs. It was Andy's mum; she had been slaving away in the kitchen all day making a beautiful casserole for the family. Andy and Josie ran down the stairs trying to barge each other out of the way as they wanted to be the first to get to the table for dinner. The smell of the casserole was making them drool, both very hungry as lunch felt like an eternity ago. "You two, stop pushing each other and sit down," shouted their mother. She was very stern and Andy and Josie both knew from the look on her face that they needed to behave. Their mother had a unique look when she was annoyed a look that could intimidate perhaps even The Dark Goblin himself.

"When will dad be home?" asked Andy.

"We have had this discussion many times Andy, when he is working in the sewers I don't know," replied his mother.

Andy shrugged his shoulders and started tucking into his casserole. It was delicious as he was so hungry, he did not realise how hot the casserole was and his mouth started to burn. He jumped up from

the table and ran to the kitchen. He stuck his mouth
under the tap in the kitchen and turned it on.

"What are you doing," bellowed this voice. It was
his dad; he had come home. Andy looked up and
turned off the tap. He ran over to his dad and gave
him a big hug. "Careful Andy, I am still dirty from
work. Let me go shower and get changed," he said.
Andy wouldn't let his dad go. He was so excited to see
him as he had been working long hours lately. "Go
have your dinner," said his dad. Andy let go of his dad
and went and sat at the table with Josie and
their mum.

"Hello dear," said their mum as their dad came
into the room and sat at the table. Andy was so
excited he wanted to ask his dad about the Goblins.

"Dad, have you seen the Goblins yet? Did you
meet The Dark Goblin?" shrieked a very excited
Andy.

"Andy what have I told you?" said his dad in a
very stern voice. Andy looked down at his bowl.

"Goblins aren't real," he replied softly.

"Exactly Goblins are not real, I do wish you
would get your head out of those stories, because that
is what they are. Nothing but stories." A very
disappointed Andy stayed quiet, he slowly started to
eat his casserole. He believed in the Goblins, and he

knew they were real and one day he was going to get the Spellmaster's book and prove to everyone that he was not making this up. He knew the real truth.

After they had finished their meal Andy headed back upstairs to his bedroom. He opened his book and looked at the images. "I will find you Dark Goblin and I will claim the Spellmaster's book and break the curse." Josie who was stood outside of Andy's bedroom slowly opened his door.

"I believe you," she said. Andy smiled, he was happy that someone finally believed him and that he was not just making things up. Josie came and sat down on the floor with Andy, they started looking at the book together. "The sewers are a maze, they go on for hundreds if not thousands of miles," said a startled Josie.

"Yes, they are. But we will find a way, we will know where to look through Dad, he has not seen them yet. The goblins are not where he has been working," Josie giggled. Andy and she knew that they could narrow down the search for the goblins. They just needed to know where to start.

"Bedtime you two," shouted their mother. Josie ran out of Andy's bedroom and headed to her own room. Andy got into bed and stared up at the ceiling. He was excited and feeling adventurous. He could not wait to head into the sewers to meet the goblins. He wanted to save them all, he wanted to help. This was his time to become a hero, much like the superhero's he had read about in his comic books. Andy closed his eyes, with his mind deep in thought and slowly fell to sleep.

2

THE SOUND OF ANDY'S ALARM WOKE HIM IN THE morning. He sat up in his bed and yawned. He looked outside and could see the sun was shining. He was thinking about the goblins and his attention kept wandering to the manhole cover in the middle of the road. He climbed out of bed and headed downstairs for breakfast. Josie, mum and dad were already sat at the table.

"Would you like some cereal?" asked mum.

"Yes please," replied Andy. Andy poured some cereal into his bowl and then got the milk. As he picked up the milk jug, he heard a voice in his head "Free us." Andy was so startled that he dropped the jug of milk onto the table. The jug bounced off the table, milk was splattered all over the floor.

"Andy what is wrong with you!" shouted dad.

"Will you pick the milk up Andy," screamed Mum. Andy shook his head and regained his focus. He could see the mess he had created. There was milk everywhere, it was a complete mess.

"Andy, clean this mess up this instant," bellowed his mum. Andy was still shocked about what he had heard. Were some of the trapped goblins trying to talk to him? Or was it just his imagination playing tricks on him? Andy headed to the cleaning cupboard and got out the mop. He started to clean up all the spilled milk on the floor. It took him ages and ages, but eventually all of the milk was mopped up. After he had cleared up, he went to see Josie who was sat in the living room, sat ready for school.

"Did you hear that voice?" he asked.

"What voice?" Josie looked very confused and Andy then realised that she could not hear this.

"It doesn't matter," replied Andy. He then headed upstairs for a shower and got himself ready for school.

The wait for the school bus seemed to take forever. Andy could not keep his eyes off the manhole cover, he was itching to go down there, in hope of finding the goblins. "Why do you keep looking at that silly old drain cover?" asked Josie.

"It is not silly, that is our way down to find the

goblins," said Andy. Then there was the sound of an engine, the smell of burning diesel filled the air. It was the school bus, late as usual. It pulled up at the side of the road and Andy and Josie stepped onto the bus for their journey to school. They sat down in their usual spaces, three seats from the back. Andy could not take his mind off the goblins he really wanted to go into the sewers to find them. Josie could see that Andy was deep in thought, she believed he was right; however, she was scared about the dangers they could face if they went into the sewers.

The bus pulled up outside the school and everyone got off. Andy and Josie headed into the main building. "Hey Billy," shouted Andy. Billy was Andy's best friend they hung out together as often as they could. They both loved the legend's stories and both wanted to prove how real they were. Billy and Andy were outsiders, they were not the popular kids, but they didn't care. Their friendship had a strong unique bond that could not be broken, by the popular kids who tried to make their lives a misery. As Andy started to head over to Billy there was a slap, it was Rick the most popular kid in school. He had tripped Andy who landed flat on his face.

"Why are you such a jerk?" shouted Josie to Rick.

"Oh, lighten up, I am just having a bit of fun,"

joked Rick who was laughing. As Andy stood up, he could see everyone stood around laughing. He felt humiliated inside, but he climbed to his feet and dusted himself off. He was not giving in to the crowd, he carried on as normal and walked up to Billy giving him a high-five.

"How was your weekend?" asked Billy.

"Not too bad, me and Josie have plans to go into the sewers and find the goblins are you coming?" said an excitable Andy.

"Yeah bro, of course I will come. Can I bring Amelia?" he asked. Amelia was Billy's girlfriend; she was also an outsider who loved to read mythical and legendary stories.

"You know Andy, she will love it?" he asked.

Andy twiddled his fingers and replied, "Well, I don't know it could be very dangerous." Suddenly a voice travelled towards them.

"Danger is my middle name." It was Amelia. She was carrying an unusual amount of books.

"What you got there?" asked Josie.

"It's a book about all sorts of mythical creatures. I am sure there is something in here about the Spellmaster's book," she said. Andy was confused.

"How do you know about the Spellmaster's book?" he asked. Billy started to step backwards and

Andy and Josie could see that he was looking somewhat uncomfortable.

"Billy told me all about the goblins and how they live in the sewers." Andy stared at Billy who was trying his best to not look Andy in the eye.

"Well, I guess it's ok. But this stays between us," said Andy. Everyone nodded and the bell sounded for class. Everyone scattered off in the direction of their classes.

Andy and Billy arrived in their science class, neither of them were interested in the lesson. "Shall we go down in the sewers this weekend?" asked Andy.

"Yes, I cannot wait," replied Billy. Their anticipation got the better of them and it was not long before the teacher cottoned on that they were not paying attention to their lesson.

"Andy and Billy, would you kindly share the chemical elements for hydrogen dioxide?" Andy and Billy looked at one another, they had not been paying attention at all to the lesson, they had no clue what the answer was.

"Sorry, sir we will listen," replied Andy. They then opened their textbooks and started to focus on the lesson. The lesson dragged on and on it seemed to last forever, until the bell went off to indicate the end of the lesson.

It was break time. Andy and Billy ran out of class and down the hallway. The popular kids were stood by their lockers sniggering and making fun of the outsiders. When they arrived in the hall they caught up with Josie and Amelie who were gossiping about the goblins. "Hey guys, we are going to go down into the sewers this weekend?" wailed a very excitable Andy. Andy then felt himself go flying across the hallway it was Rick. He had grabbed Andy and pulled him away.

"Are you trying to get me in trouble, you snitched on me about that trip earlier? YOU got me detention," he shouted. Andy began to shake with fear, a small crowd gathered round shouting "fight, fight." Andy was not a fighter; he was pushed up against the wall and he clenched his eyes tight shut waiting for the inevitable punch.

"What is going on here?" shouted a voice from down the hall. It was the principal. Rick let go of Andy and put his arm around him.

"Nothing miss, just catching up with an old friend." The principal glared at Rick.

"Is this the case?" she asked Andy.

"Yes miss, we were just chatting," replied Andy who was still trembling. He did not want any more trouble from Rick.

"Right, everyone back to class," shouted the principal. With that everyone scattered off to their next lessons.

Andy was quiet for the rest of the day and when school ended, he and Josie got the bus home. Andy hated Rick for what he had done to him today. He couldn't understand who had reported Rick for tripping him up. When they got home, Andy headed to his bedroom. He lay on his bed and started to scream into his pillow.

Shortly after Josie came in his room, "it's ok Andy, Rick is a jerk." Andy sat up on his bed, his eyes red from where he had been crying.

"I know," he said. As the day drew on, they were waiting for Dad to come home from work. It was now 10pm and there was no sign of Dad. "Mum did Dad say he was working overnight?" asked Andy.

"No, he did not, but I am sure that he will be home soon," replied mum. Without thinking too much into it, Andy headed upstairs and got into bed.

The following morning Andy went downstairs to see his mum and Josie on the phone, they were trying to call dad. However, he was not answering his phone. "Is everything ok?" asked Andy. Josie ran over to Andy.

"Dad did not come from work yesterday; he still

is not home now, and we cannot get in touch with him." Andy gasped and immediately thought about the goblins. Had the goblins captured his dad, were they keeping him prisoner in the sewers?

He whispered to Josie, "The goblins could have him there trapped."

Josie looked very stern. "This is no silly laughing matter our dad and his colleagues have not come home." Andy sat down on the chair at the table. He knew that something had happened with the goblins and his dad, he needed to go down, and deep into the sewers to find out what was going on.

3

THERE WAS A LARGE NEWS PRESENCE ON THE missing workers in the sewers. It was all over the news, on the TV and people were in shock that four people could go missing down there. Andy wanted to know exactly where his dad had been working, so he could head down into the sewers with his friends and find his dad and help break the curse. "Josie, we are going to go in the morning, on Saturday about 3am. I am going to text Billy now to let him know." Josie was scared she had deep concerns that this was not a smart idea, if four adults went missing down there, what chance did four teenagers have?

"I don't think that is a smart idea," she whispered. "Mum is still very anxious about dad. It is not safe down there it could be a flood or something even more dangerous." Andy rolled his eyes.

"You told me you believed in the goblins; we both know that they are the reason behind all of this!" Josie knew she did not have a choice and that Andy was going to go down there anyway. To stop him from getting lost or being foolish she knew she would have to go along to support him and to keep him out of trouble.

School that day was very quiet, some of the other children had their parents missing in the sewers and the atmosphere was very solemn. Even the popular kids were quiet, it was so eerie and very strange indeed. Even the teachers did not appear interested in teaching the lessons. "Today is really strange," Andy said to Billy whilst they were on lunch.

"Totally weird bro. My English teacher just stared into space for a whole hour," replied Billy. Amelia and Josie then came over and sat down. "I think the people disappearing in the sewers has got everyone confused and worried," said Josie.

"Maybe, or maybe not, but what if The Dark Goblin has cast a spell on people. Maybe they are under his spell?" said Amelie.

"That does not make any sense," said Andy.

"Why doesn't it?" replied Amelie.

"Because not everyone is acting strange," Andy wailed.

"I agree," said Josie. Amelia simply looked down at her lunch and began eating with the others. What Amelia had said really made Andy think, were some people really under a spell? cast by The Dark Goblin from the Spellmaster's book?

As the school day came to a close, they could see Rick was his usual self, pushing past the other kids and not giving a care in the world for their feelings. He was such a typical bully, but yet he was idolised by all the popular kids. "What you doing outsiders" bellowed Rick from across the hallway.

"Nothing that requires your attention," scowled Josie. Josie was not scared of Rick at all, he did not intimidate her in any way.

"I have my eye on you lot!" shouted Rick in a very angry voice. He stormed off down the hallway. There was hardly any sign of the teachers.

"What is going on?" asked Billy sounding deeply concerned.

"I told you it's a spell," replied Amelia in a very sarcastic tone. It was Friday afternoon and school was now out for the weekend. They all started to head home with the plan to enter the sewers at 3am.

"Mum, where was dad working last?" asked Andy.

"He told me he was working under the old dockyards," Mum replied. Andy's eyes lit up he now knew where to start. He ran upstairs and turned on his computer. He frantically searched the internet for a map or blueprints of the sewers. After twenty minutes of looking he grinned. He had found an old map by the construction workers who had built the sewers. He picked up his mobile phone and texted Billy telling him that he could find the way. He printed off the map and ran to Josie's room where she was playing her videogames. "Josie" shouted Andy.

"Not now, I have almost finished this level," she wailed.

"This can't wait look." Josie turned her head to look at what Andy was holding, then looked back at the screen.

"ANDY, you cost me that level," she shouted very annoyed.

"I have a map of the sewers, well it is an old map, but it will work. I know that dad was last working under the old dockyard."

The old dockyard was disused, no one had been working at that dockyard for almost 50 years. However, the sewers ran right beneath them. It was a perfect spot for people to hide, perhaps even hide an entire goblin army underneath it. The buildings in the dockyard were all overgrown and it had been put up for auction many times in the past, yet no one ever seemed interested in buying it. Andy knew that there was something unusual, about this dockyard for as long as he could remember. It was the only part of the town that no birds would fly over. It was very green with a lot of overgrowth and many of the buildings had the roofs collapsed in on them. Andy remembered all this when he and Billy went to see the dockyard a few months back, but they were chased away by an angry workman who was putting up a keep out fence.

"Well, how far is that from the manhole cover?" she asked. Andy paused and looked at the map, he started to make some calculations in his head.

"Hmmmm, about three miles," he said sounding unsure.

"Three miles that could take us hours and that is if we don't get lost."

Andy was convinced that things would go smoothly. He showed Josie the map and made sure she felt comfortable with how things would go. As the sunset they both went to bed. Andy set his alarm for 2:30am. He was so excited that he struggled to get to sleep. He wanted to find his dad, yet he wanted to meet the goblins. As he lay there awake in bed, he thought to himself. Am I the boy? The one to finally break the curse of the Dark Goblin.

Andy continued to toss and turn, but his mind was way too active. He could not get the idea out of his head about what was going to happen. He wasn't scared, he was excited. He kept having the vision of holding The Spellmaster's book, breaking the curse, freeing all the goblins. He could see The Dark Goblin before him surrendering and disappearing back into the underworld from where he once came. Before he knew it, his alarm was going off. It was 2:30am. He jumped out of bed quickly and then crept to Josie's room.

"It's time," he whispered. He could hear Josie getting out of bed. Andy went back into his bedroom and got dressed. He grabbed a flashlight out of his bedside drawer and headed downstairs. He snuck out the back door and waited for Josie to arrive.

"Boo." Andy jumped out of his skin. Josie had snuck up on him.

"That was not cool, Josie," moaned Andy.

"Oh, lighten up," she joked. Josie was dressed in all dark clothing she looked like a ninja.

"Why are you dressed all in black?" asked Andy.

"Well, why not, it is dark down there and it will

make me harder to see," she replied. Andy rolled his eyes and shook his head.

"Really, these are goblins that live in the darkness. Do you really think that they will struggle to see you? They will be used to seeing in the dark. Plus, if their eyesight is not that good then they will definitely be able to hear you." Josie gulped and started to look a bit sheepish.

"Well, that is a risk I am going to have to take," she said. "Any way let's get going." They both started to walk towards the main road and eventually arrived at the manhole cover. They stood and checked the time. All they had to do now was to wait for Billy and Amelia to arrive.

4

THE WAIT FOR BILLY AND AMELIA WAS INTENSE. Andy was stood with Josie by the manhole cover making sure that there was no traffic around. At 3am Billy and Amelia arrived.

"Where are your flashlights?" asked Andy.

"We have them in our backpacks," replied Billy. Andy looked at the manhole cover and realised that this was not going to come off so easily.

"Well how do we lift this?" joked Josie. Andy started to think, then as if a light bulb lit up in his mind, he had an idea. His dad had a crowbar in the shed.

"Wait here, I will be right back," he said. Andy then ran off down the road to his house. He ran around the back of the house and into the shed. He grabbed the crowbar and headed back to the manhole cover. He lodged the tip of the crowbar into the manhole.

"Right Billy push with me." Andy and Billy both grabbed the crowbar and pushed down as hard as they could. The manhole cover started to budge. Josie and Amelia than grabbed the manhole cover and together all 4 of them lifted it off. Below was nothing, but darkness.

"Let's do this," said Andy. Everyone just stared down into the dark abyss, not knowing what they were about to step into.

"Well who goes first then?" asked Andy.

"Well this is all your idea so how about you go first," replied Josie who had an enormous grin on her face.

"Very well," replied Andy. He turned on his torch and shone it down the hole. He could see the flow of shallow water below. He grabbed onto the maintenance ladder and slowly headed down into the sewer. His feet touched the water, which barely covered the soles of his shoes.

"Ok guys, come on down," he yelled. He could hear his voice echo, back to him as he called out. One by one the others slowly came down the ladder into the sewer.

"Ewww this is disgusting, it stinks!" said Josie who had pinched her nose to stop the smell of the sewer from making her feel sick. Amelia let out a slight giggle with Billy.

"Well it is a sewer," joked Andy.

Andy pulled out the map, he used his torch to see where they were and where they needed to go.

"Follow me," he said, loudly hearing his echo return back to him. Slowly, they made their way in single file with Andy leading at the front followed by Josie, Billy and finally Amelia. Andy was very heavy footed and extremely noisy. Amelia was deeply concerned with this as she had read in many books that goblins were very sensitive to sound.

"I think we should all be a bit quieter," exclaimed Amelia.

"Yes, we don't want to draw attention to ourselves," whispered Billy. They slowly tiptoed down the long sewage pathway, barely making a splash in the stinking water beneath their feet. Josie would continuously shine the torch at her feet. She was so grossed out by the stench, that she did not want anything disgusting to be stuck to her trainers.

After what seemed like an eternity, they arrived at a four-way junction. Andy stopped and looked at his map. He was now very confused; this junction was not on his map.

"Well Andy, which way?" asked Josie. Andy was still very confused, he had no idea which way to go, but he did not want the others to know that he could get everyone lost.

Then without hesitation he said, "we go left." Everyone followed Andy into the deep dark sewer. Andy kept telling himself that he hoped he was right. But then would also think what if he was wrong? They could all end up lost down there in the sewers. As they walked deeper into the sewers the sound of something or rats could be heard scurrying in the distance.

"I hate rats," wailed Josie.

"So do I," replied Billy. They could all hear what they thought were rats, but they could not see any. As they walked further and deeper down the passageway the sound of scurrying intensified.

"I do not like the sound of this," cried Josie, she was now becoming increasingly concerned as the noise intensified.

"It is fine, let's keep going," said Andy who was

being stubborn. They had come so far, why give up now? As they kept walking a rat brushed past Josie's feet.

She screamed out, "that is it let's get out of here!"

"No," shouted Andy. Andy then stopped, in the distance, it looked as if the whole floor of the sewer was moving.

"I need another torch," he called. Billy passed him a torch. Andy shone both the torches in the distance. There were hundreds if not thousands of rats scurrying towards them. He felt his knees tremble, but there was nothing that they could do.

The rats ran through everyone, causing all four of them to scream out. It was like a stampede seen in a safari. After a few minutes, all the rats had passed. Everyone stood still in shock they let out a huge sigh. Andy then started to walk as they continued; they could see some red marks, what were they? As they got closer, they could see they were droplets of blood on the sewer walls.

"What is this?" Andy thought to himself. As they continued on their journey, they started to notice the dead rats on the floor. They had been partially eaten!

"Goblins," Andy wailed. Then suddenly there was a high-pitched scream which echoed down the passageway. Andy shone his torch in the distance, what he saw sent shivers down his spine. A blacked - out silhouette of a small ghastly figure, it had large pointed ears to the side and appeared to be wearing some kind of cloak. It was crouched down and was eating something. Perhaps a rat, Andy was not sure. Suddenly something had landed at Andy's feet. It was a half-eaten rat. They had been spotted, the figure stood up and all Andy could see was these eyes staring at him through the darkness. They were a deep red like a demon from hell. He felt his heart starting to race. There was a huge cackle and then the silhouette vanished. Everyone screamed and turned around starting to run back. They ran as fast as they could back to the ladder and climbed up out of the sewer.

"Don't ask us to go back in there," cried Josie. Her heart racing from the ear-piercing cackle that had frightened the life out of everyone. Andy felt defeated, but what he saw gave him the biggest fright of his life. He now knew the goblins were real, and they were not just some silly myth and made-up story. For the first time, he felt weak, that he was too afraid to try and take on the goblin army and The Dark Goblin.

"We need a better plan," Andy said to the others.

"Agreed," replied Amelia, Billy nodded in acknowledgement. Josie, however, was deeply concerned about the dangers that would follow. However, she wanted her dad back as much as Andy did and knew that eventually, they would return, but return better equipped and ready to face the goblins that lurked in the sewer.

5

Sunday arrived, Andy could not shake the vision of the creature that he saw in the sewer from his mind. He knew in his head it was a goblin. He went onto his computer to see what he could use that would be effective against goblins. He found that they have an elemental weakness to ice, but how could he use this to his advantage. He looked through his desk drawers and found his old catapult. Then the brainwave commenced. He would freeze blocks of ice, and he would use them with his slingshot. Yet he had to find a way to keep the blocks of ice cool. He ran downstairs and rummaged through the kitchen hoping to find something useful. He came across some of old cold food storage boxes, they used when they went camping. He took the ice packs out and filled them with water before placing them in the freezer. He was now going to be armed and ready.

"Andy do you really think small blocks of ice will work? I mean they live in the sewers maybe they are scared of light?" Andy smiled from ear to ear.

"Brilliant Josie." He went into the shed and looked for the most powerful torches they had.

"This could work," he said. Andy packed away the high-powered torches, he texted Billy to tell him that this time they would be armed and ready. Shortly after recieved a phone call from Billy, who asked why they needed to enter the sewers on the main road and why not just enter them at the old dockyard? Andy felt a bit stupid; this was the most logical thing they could have done the first time, yet he never even gave it a thought. After the phone call he told Josie that they would go to the sewers again; but enter through the old dockyard.

"Not today though," said Josie.

"Of course not, the ice is not ready. We will go in a few days when we are all prepared to face the goblins head on." Josie was still concerned and did not like the idea. She heard how the goblin was crunching through the rat that it was eating. Bones that crunch like that in someone's mouth would usually indicate razor-sharp teeth. The idea of that frightened her to the core.

Josie could not get the vision out of her head, she hated rats and thought they were horrible disgusting creatures. Yet there was this feeling of sadness overcoming her. She actually started to feel sorry for the rats, only being down there in the sewers as food for the nasty goblins. She had to take her mind off it, otherwise she knew she would just give herself nightmares all night. She started to think. "What could I ask Andy?" then it clicked.

"Andy what is so important about the Spellmaster's book?" asked Josie. This was music to Andy's ears he could now tell the tale of The Spellmaster.

"Let me tell you a story Josie." Josie started to wish she hadn't asked, but she was keen to learn about why it was so very important.

"Centuries ago, there was a powerful magician, he could cast any spells that he wanted. He could turn people into anything with his spells. He could even influence the minds of people. He became so powerful that he locked away all the other legends and trapped them. Until one day when he was out looking for items to create a new spell to cast away all the evil in the world, a little old goblin snuck into his home. He stole the book and when he touched it, he became larger in size and more youthful. He was a clever goblin, and he managed to use The Spellmaster's own spell against him, casting him away. When this happened many of the legends woke from their slumber. They are lying in wait ready to strike when the time is right. The Goblin then cursed the book for anyone who tried to steal it to turn into a goblin that would become part of his army."

"Wow that is some story, but if we try and take the book won't we also become goblins?" asked Josie.

"Well, maybe yes. But legend has it that one day a boy will be the chosen one who is immune to the curse. The legend states that this boy will take the book from The Dark Goblin breaking the curse and freeing all of those under his spell." Josie was intrigued.

"That is good, but what happens to The Dark Goblin?" she asked.

Andy let out a deep breath and replied, "the legend does not say." A concerned Josie remained quiet; she was not convinced that her brother Andy was the chosen one. He could not even put his washing in the washing basket, let alone break a curse! She started to chuckle when she started to think how hopeless he was around the house.

"What is so funny?" scowled Andy.

"Oh, nothing," sniggered Josie. Andy just rolled his eyes, he knew that Josie was just making fun of him, but he was not going to bite back. He wanted to find out as much information as he could.

Andy went back to his computer and started to look at images on the internet of goblins. He was trying to find something that resembled the silhouetted figure of what was staring right back at him. He would click through many images lizard man, troglodyte, but no goblins. Then he stumbled across an old photograph that had a date under the image. April 19th, 1949. The image was a dark figure so similar in shape to what he had seen.

"Josie look, there it is. That is the proof, people have taken photographs from over 60 years ago and that is what I saw." Josie came over to the computer and took a long deep look at the image.

"So, do you think that they live forever, cursed to be his prisoner until the spell is broken?" Andy continued to read the attached information to the photograph.

"Yes, I think that might be right, which means we have to break this curse. All these poor souls trapped inside these horrible skins. We need to free them," he cried.

"Will breaking the curse, free The Spellmaster?" asked Josie.

"Yes, it should, but I would not worry The Spellmaster was always known as a hero, he never used his powers or spells to try and take over the world. He used them to try and keep the monsters away." Andy replied. A huge sigh of relief came out of Josie. She did not really want to take on one monster to only awaken another. At least now they had more understanding of what they were going up against. Next time they would be more prepared to take on the goblins.

Andy rang Billy and told him to get some ice and make sure he had a way to use this to their advantage, he explained about his catapult.

"Make sure you tell Amelia everything I told you," said Andy on the phone. He had got his confidence back and felt that he was prepared to take on anything that came his way. He checked on his ice cubes to make sure that they were freezing the way they should be.

"Andy if you keep opening the freezer, they will not freeze at all," explained Josie. Andy closed the door to the freezer and headed upstairs. The plan was ready, but did he really know what he was getting himself and the others into..........?

6

It was back to school for the week. Andy woke and did not want to get up, he looked at his alarm clock and switched it off. He lay back down on his bed, but something kept him awake. He could hear his mum sobbing away in her bedroom. He pulled himself out of bed and crept down the hallway to his parent's room. He stood by the door and could hear his mum's cries. He slowly opened the door and could see his mum crying into her pillow. She was clearly concerned for his dad. Andy stepped away from the door. He could feel the rage flowing through his veins.

"Those horrible goblins," he said to himself. He then turned back to the bedroom and whispered softly, "Don't worry mum I will bring dad back."

After heading downstairs there was no breakfast made, mum was still upstairs in her bedroom. Josie had taken it upon herself to make her own toast.

"Well, where is mine?" asked Andy.

"You know where the bread is. Make it yourself," scowled Josie. She really did not like being told what to do, especially by Andy who would always place demands upon her as and when he chose to. A disgruntled Andy made his way to the bread bin and got himself some bread. He put it in the toaster and kept tutting as he went along.

"You can tut all you like Andy, but I am not your servant," joked Josie. Andy felt annoyed, he felt he always helped Josie when she wanted help, and yet she wouldn't do such a simple task for him. Andy made his toast and sat down at the table. He really did not want to go to school today. All he wanted to do was to bring his family back together and end the curse that The Dark Goblin had placed.

The journey to school was quiet, Andy was still annoyed at Josie for not helping him out and just leaving him to sort out everything for himself. They both remained silent, even when they arrived at school, they did not interact with one another. Yet they still walked side by side. They met up with Billy and Amelia, who could instantly tell that there was some animosity between Andy and Josie. Their body language gave away a lot. Both had their arms folded and would keep looking down.

"Come on guys, whatever it is sort it out now," said Billy.

"What makes you think something is up?" implied Andy.

"Hey, we were not born yesterday," replied Amelia who then started to giggle. Amelia's giggle set off Andy and Josie, and they both begun to laugh.

"Yeah this is stupid," said Andy. Josie continued to laugh, and then she gave her brother a hug.

"See that was not so bad was it?" said Billy. They all then started to walk in to school. As they walked in people seemed back to their old selves. They were being stared at by the popular kids who would make silly noises or shout insults in their direction.

Josie could not stand the insults, so she shouted out, "bite me." A locker then slammed.

"What did you say?" shouted Rick. Josie was not going to back down from Rick.

"I said bite me," she shouted back. Rick started to storm over with a very quick march in Josie's direction. Andy took this as an opportunity to finally get his own back, as Rick was marching Andy stretched out his leg. Rick not seeing this caught his foot on Andy's leg and fell face-down onto the floor.

"Arghhh" she said letting out a massive breath.

Everyone started to laugh in the hallway, even the popular kids were laughing at Rick now. Chants of "you got tripped by an outsider," started to echo down the corridors. Rick was not amused. He pulled himself up to his feet. He walked over to Andy and looked down at him with such a cold stare that it made Andy's heart shudder.

"You're going to pay for that!" said Rick. Andy felt the chill run down his spine, Rick was not shouting nor was he loud in any way. But his facial expression and tone of voice implied that Andy better be careful. Rick stormed off down the hallway to his class. Shortly after the bell rang for first lesson. It was time for Andy and Josie to head to Maths a subject that they both loved.

Andy was always good at problem solving, Josie was always good with numbers. Together they were very strong at maths. They loved the lessons that much that they actually paid attention during them. However, on this occasion, they wanted to talk more about how they were going to infiltrate the old dockyards. They had heard that on the side of the docks there was a large opening that walked them directly into the sewers. This was music to their ears as there would be light on this tunnel. This also meant that they did not have to worry about carrying that awful heavy crowbar all the way to the old dockyard.

"This time, we go in daylight," pleaded Josie.

"Yes, we will. I read that creatures that live in darkness would be very vulnerable to the light. Which means we could draw them towards it."

"Quiet you two, focus on your work," yelled the maths teacher from across the room. Andy had been busted yet again, in a lesson not focusing on his work. This started to make him worry about his school report. What would mum think? Or dad if he were to ever come back home.

Andy just knew that he was being held captive by the goblins, and he started to see that Josie was actually beginning to believe him also.

"We will talk on break and lunch," whispered Andy, he really did not want to get in trouble anymore. He wanted to make sure that he did not disappoint his parents when his report would be released. Being busted twice in one week, really was beginning to scare him. He managed to finish all his work in the lesson and started to feel a little better in himself. The bell rang and it was time for lunch. Now he could talk to Josie and the others about his plan.

It seemed to take forever to get through the queues for lunch. Andy was starting to get frustrated, as he needed time to talk to everyone about the plan. After waiting for about fifteen minutes he managed to get served. He quickly grabbed his lunch of ham and potatoes and ran to find the others. Andy ran across the hall and sat down at the table. Josie just stared at his food.

"What is that?" she asked.

"Oh, I don't know, I don't care either, I just needed to talk to you guys about the plan?" he said it so quickly in excitement that it took the others a few minutes to process.

"Ok, you all know about the ice. So we are going to enter through the old dockyard. Down the north side, there is a small drop if you drop down here there is an entrance to the sewer. This time we are going in daylight. I think the goblins might be vulnerable to light, so this could work for us." Everyone just stared at Andy.

"I think you need to lay off the sugar," joked Billy.

"No time for jokes, we are going to do this." Andy was still so excited and just to keep him quiet everyone agreed with him.

A voice from behind them echoed, "Are you really going down there, well thanks for letting me know." It was Rick, he then stood up and turned around to face them all. "Watch your back, I haven't forgotten about what happened." He then walked away with his food tray with a huge grin on his face.

"Well that is just brilliant, now he knows our plan," said Josie. She was clearly annoyed and infuriated. "Why do you always have to be so loud?" pointing at Andy. Andy just placed his head in his hands.

"How was I to know he was there?" he said quietly.

"It's the cafeteria doofus, its full of people," scowled Amelia. Billy remained quiet, then he had a thought.

"Hey, wait. We never said a day. He had no idea what day or what time we are going. We just said daylight. He won't hang around there all day on his own." Josie rolled her eyes.

"This is Rick, he is the stupidest guy in the world. He will just stand there for a week if it meant he could get his hands on Andy for tripping him."

"Thanks for reminding me," replied Andy his voice croaky with fear. He did not want to be on the receiving end of a beating from Rick.

7

THE WEEK WENT REALLY FAST AND SOON IT WAS the weekend once again. Andy and Josie's dad had still not returned and the searches by the police in the sewers came up with nothing. People had started to lose hope that anyone could be found alive now as it had been so long since they had gone missing. Andy was packed, armed and ready to head back in the sewers. This time things were going to go to plan. There was a knock on his bedroom door. It was Josie.

"Are you ready to do this?" she asked.

"Never been more ready," replied Andy. He grabbed his backpack and headed downstairs with Josie.

"Mum we are going out, we will be back later," he

shouted as they both scurried out the front door. The sun was out and the day was bright.

"This could be used to our advantage" said Andy. Josie looked around.

"Yes, it is very bright. What a beautiful day," she exclaimed. They were meeting both Billy and Amelia in town. Then together they would all walk to the old dockyard.

The town was quiet, it was still quite early in the morning. They arrived at the meeting spot, the large mermaid fountain in the town centre. Billy and Amelia were already waiting. This was a shock for Andy as he always usually had to wait for Billy to arrive. Billy was usually late for everything.

"Did you wet the bed or something bro?" joked Andy.

"Ha ha. Very funny," replied Billy.

"Let's get a move on, we want to wrap this up quickly," said an unimpressed Amelia.

"Ok, let's do this then," replied Andy. They all started walking, this time they were walking tall. Feeling confident that they would now have the upper hand and that nothing in that sewer could scare them like it did the last time. The walk to the old dockyard seemed to take forever. They would often see the seagulls flying above them.

"Surely we are close now? There are seagulls everywhere," wailed Josie. Andy rolled his eyes.

"You have been saying that for the last half an hour. Another few minutes," he replied.

A few short minutes later they arrived at the large perimeter fence that had been erected around the old dockyard. There were large signs all over the fence saying Danger keep out.

"I really do not like the look of this," cried Josie.

"Josie, it is just standard practice they have to put these signs up or everyone would just always walk in," replied Andy. Billy and Amelia had a good look at the fence. It was very high and very strong.

"How do you think we get through this?" asked Billy. Andy was unsure. He walked up and down the fence, grabbing it in places and giving it a slight tug. Then he spotted something, one of the clips on the fence that was holding the sections together was broken.

"Hey guys, come over here," shouted Andy. Everyone scurried over to where Andy was stood.

"We can get in here, help me lift the panel and we may be able to move it enough to squeeze through." Everyone grabbed a part of the fence. Andy grabbed the edges of the fence.

"Ok guys...1....2....3...go," called out Andy.

Everyone lifted as much as they could, but the fence was far too heavy for them to lift.

"What do you suggest we do now?" asked Billy. Then suddenly a very familiar voice from behind them spoke.

"You wimps, get out of the way."

There he was, Rick stood behind them. "How did you know we were here?" asked Josie. Rick looked down at everyone.

"I followed you, and I also said watch your back." Andy gulped he was now very scared. There were no teachers to protect him here, and he did not know what Rick was going to do to him. Rick walked straight up to Andy and pushed him gently to the side. He then grabbed the fence and managed to lift it slightly, everyone else then grabbed a part of the fence and helped Rick lift the fence out of the support creating enough of a gap for everyone to squeeze through.

One by one they squeezed through the gap. Strangely Rick followed on behind them.

"Why are you following us?" bellowed Josie.

"I heard about these so-called goblins and I want to see for myself if they are real," he replied. A confused Andy finally spoke.

"Why do you care so much?" he asked. It then

looked as if Rick was about to cry. His eyes started to fill, and he started to look emotional for the first time ever.

"Many years ago, me and my little brother were playing in this very dockyard. We were playing a game called hide-and-seek. We were taking it in turns, when it was my turn to find my brother I went and stood behind the old boathouse. I had to count to twenty which I did. I then called out saying ready or not here I come. When I went to look for him, I could not find him anywhere. I dropped down the ledge to the entrance of the sewer and I heard him scream. It was such a loud scream that it hurt my ears. I ran into the sewer as fast as I could, I ran down the left corridor following the sounds of his screams. Then suddenly I was thrown back by this blue light. It lifted me off my feet and sent me crashing to the floor. When I sat up there was a large shadow. It looked like he was carrying a book. It cackled at me and then ran off. I ran out of the sewer in fear and have never been back in. No one believed me about what I saw. Then the other day at lunch I heard you guys talking about it. So here I am. I want to find out what happened to my little brother."

Everyone was shocked by what they heard. Andy started to think this may be the reason, that Andy is always a jerk. Because he has not been able to find peace with what has happened to his brother. Suddenly Andy started to feel empathetic towards Rick.

"I am so sorry to hear that. Our dad went missing in here last week," replied Andy. Rick put his hands in his pocket, he clearly felt awkward after talking about his missing brother. But it was nice to see the emotional and loving side of Rick as everyone assumed, he was just robotic with no emotions inside him whatsoever.

"You said that this creature was carrying a book that must be The Dark Goblin. He carries the Spellmaster's book. The blue light that lifted and threw you back would have been one of his magic spells," Andy said.

"Maybe, but what you said in the cafeteria about what you saw reminded me of this creature just a slightly smaller version." Andy was concerned The Dark Goblin was larger than the monster he had seen then maybe he would be too powerful.

"This Spellmaster's Book. What is it?" asked Rick.

"Legend has it that this book has been cursed by The Dark Goblin and that anyone who tries to steal it becomes a goblin and becomes one of his minions."

"So, what you are saying is that my brother could still be alive?" yelled Rick.

"Maybe yes, but the book makes The Dark Goblin very powerful only the chosen one can defeat him," replied Andy. Rick did not care about no chosen one. He wanted his brother back and nothing was going to stop him.

"I will pound that creature into next week," boasted Rick. Andy could see Josie rolling her eyes. He also knew it was a stupid thing to say. They had no idea how formidable The Dark Goblin could be.

"So which way is it to this entrance then," asked Josie.

"Follow me," said Rick. Rick took the lead and started to move some of the overgrowth. There was so much plant life that had started to grow through the cracks in the concrete. A few old rusty boats could be seen, and the smell of rust was very intense. They slowly made their way past the old cranes. They were massive and still standing even though the amount of rust on the steel supports looked like they should have just collapsed already.

"This place is like a graveyard!" said Josie. Billy and Amelia were holding hands. They were quite scared by their surroundings, but they did not want to tell anyone about this. As they walked past the cranes, they noticed some bones on the ground. Andy knelt down and picked up one of the bones.

"Are those human?" whimpered Josie. Andy looked at the bone.

"I don't think so," he said. "Looks like some kind of animal maybe a cat?" he replied. Andy put the bone back down, and they continued to follow Rick. They stepped down onto a ledge, and they all turned around. There it was, the large circular entrance. The light was only shining for the first few metres into the sewer.

"Everyone ready," said Andy. They all stared deep into the sewer before taking their first steps.

8

THEY SLOWLY STEPPED FOOT INTO THE
entrance, making their way into the darkness slowly
step by step. Andy made sure his ice blocks were still
frozen. He had his catapult ready in case of any
surprises. The sewer was eerily quiet, nothing could
be heard apart from the sound of dripping water,
which could be seen dripping from the roof of the
sewer. The stench was unbearable.

"This part smells even worse than the last part we
were in," said Andy. Josie who was pinching her nose
just shook her head. She hated bad smells and this
was definitely her idea of hell. The five of them slowly
made their way forward. It was so dark it was pitch
black so much so they could not see a thing. Andy
pulled out his high-powered torch and shone it into

the distance. The sewer was that long that he still could not see an end even with his torch. However, it illuminated the area they were in and about one hundred metres very well.

"Good, we have excellent vision," said Billy. Rick clenched his fist.

"Yes, I cannot wait to get my hands on these slimy creeps," he said. Josie still unimpressed by Rick's confidence and had enough.

"You really think you stand a chance in a fight against one of them? They have razor-sharp teeth. You did not see how it tore that rat apart whilst it was eating it," she said.

"I don't care, about its teeth it has to bite me first," said an irritated Rick.

They slowly continued down the passageway.

"Ssshhhh," said Andy. "Do you hear that?" Everyone stopped and listened. In the distance, the faint sound of laughter could be heard.

"That has to be them?" said Amelia. Everyone remained deadly quiet and slowly walked forward, being very careful where they placed their feet. Then there was a crack, Josie had stepped on an old branch that had made its way into the sewer.

"Quiet" scowled Andy, but it was too late. The laughter got louder and the sound of footsteps in the water moving at speed could be heard. Andy aimed his torch forward and there it was a goblin heading their way. It was green in colour and had deep dark eyes. It was carrying an axe and it had a menacing smile on its face.

"Get back!" shouted Andy. Amelia, Billy, and Josie stood behind Andy and Rick. Andy quickly reached into his bag and pulled out some ice cubes. He put one in his catapult and fired it in the direction of the charging goblin. He missed; the goblin started to laugh.

"You really think you can hurt me!" cackled the goblin.

"What they can talk?" said a shocked Andy. The others were all in a state of shock, they could not believe that this monster could talk. Rick took a stance and stood his ground, ready to fight the goblin. Andy grabbed a few more chunks of ice and put them all into his catapult. He shot in the direction of the goblin and then there was a loud crash. The goblin crashed to the floor.

"Curse you," it wailed. Andy and Rick ran over to the goblin. The ice had caused him to burn severely. Rick grabbed the goblin and pulled it up.

"Where is my brother? you disgusting thing!" he shouted. The goblin started to laugh again and then proceeded to spit green slime in Rick's face. Rick threw the goblin down on the floor and the goblin started to dissolve as it was vanishing into nothing, but green slime it could be heard saying "He will get you all."

"That was so gross," wailed Josie. Amelia knelt down and put her hand in the slime.

"It is gross, but it is also fascinating. The ice can kill them." Andy smiled, perhaps the ice could defeat The Dark Goblin. He now felt so confident that he could defeat The Dark Goblin that his worries and anxieties just faded away. Billy stepped over the slime to catch up.

"So how many more of these do you think there are?" he asked.

"I don't know, and I don't care. They will all die," said Rick. Josie then jumped in front of Rick.

"No, one of these could be my dad, we need to try and help them." Rick went to push Josie aside until…

"Listen, Rick, one of these could also be your brother." Rick stopped and dropped his hands to his side.

"Very well, but who did we just kill?" he asked. Amelia who was still examining the slimy remains picked up something.

"This is a coin," she yelled. "It's from 1956," she said. Well that cannot be anyone we know" replied Andy. "Let's keep going" whispered Billy. They all then turned their attention to the never-ending passageway that was set out before them. This place was a real maze of twists and turns.

As they pushed on, they could see so many dead rats, all with bite marks on them clearly visible.

"This is so gross, why do they eat the rats?" asked Josie.

"Quiet, there could be more of them down here," said Andy. The water started to get a little deeper and very soon it was over their ankles.

"Ewwwww," wailed Josie. Amelia started to laugh.

"You should have worn boots like I have," Josie shone her torch in Amelia's face.

"Don't get smart with me," she shouted. She then scowled at Amelia.

"I was only joking," replied Amelia.

"Ssshhh, we need to keep moving now isn't the time or the place," called Andy.

Cackles in the distance were more apparent now, however, there were many. It sounded like there was much more than just the one goblin this time. As they finally reached the end of the passageway, they could see a small gap in the wall. There was some light that shone through the gap. Andy peered through the gap and gasped in horror.

"What is it?" asked Billy. Andy was frozen he could not talk; he was shocked by what he had seen. Billy peered through the gap.

"Oh my," he whispered. It was an enormous square area with many tunnels leading off it. In the room, there were hundreds of goblins. An army like they did not expect. There were torches made with fire. The goblins clearly were not stupid and had learned to live and thrive in the darkness. Everyone else then took turns in looking through the gap. When they all had taken a look, they felt deflated.

"Well now what?" said Josie. Andy who had now come to his senses started to think of a plan, but nothing was coming to mind. They were heavily outnumbered and truly did not stand a chance if they went into that room.

"I think we need to retreat," said Andy.

"No way, we have come this far! I want to find my brother," bellowed Rick in a deep tone.

"We will not survive there are too many," said Andy. Rick was infuriated, he grabbed Andy and forced him up against the wall.

"We are not leaving here until I find my little

brother." Andy had heard enough he finally had the courage and pushed Rick back.

"No, it is too dangerous" he shouted. Forgetting himself for a minute he did not realise how loud he was. The sound of "we are not alone" could be heard coming through the gap. They had alerted the goblins to their presence. Everyone started to look at one another. What were they going to do now?

9

"Let's get out of here," shouted Billy and Amelia at the same time. They started to run off back down the long passageway.

"Guys wait," shouted Andy. As Billy and Amelia were running a goblin jumped out in front of them. The stopped and turned around only to another goblin behind them. Billy opened his bag and threw all his ice at one of the goblins. The goblin started to melt; however, he had no ice left for the goblin behind him. Billy and Amelia grabbed onto each other holding one another they closed their eyes waiting to meet their fate. Then they heard a bang, they opened their eyes and Rick was fighting the goblin. Rick forced the goblin up against the wall. He managed to restrain it. Andy came running over and grabbed an ice cube. As the goblin went to spit at Rick. Andy shoved the ice cube in its mouth, causing its head to melt away. The slime went all over Rick's hands.

"Yuck, this is really not nice," he said.

"I am impressed," echoed this terrifying voice from down the passageway. Everyone froze and Andy turned to the direction of the voice. He shone his torch down the passageway. Everyone gasped out, a goblin but no ordinary goblin. This goblin was much bigger, and he was carrying an old antique-looking brown book. He had lone pointy ears one of which had a large ring in it. Behind him were many goblins waiting for his command. They were salivating. It was dripping from their mouths, and they looked very hungry. Everyone was terrified this was not a goblin, you could face hand-to-hand. Andy quickly pulled out his catapult and shot some ice at the goblin. The ice hit the goblin's chest and fell to the floor.

"Hahaha," laughed the goblin.

"You really think you can hurt me with that?" Andy looked at Rick for help.

"What do we do?" asked Andy.

Without thinking Rick ran towards the goblin.

"I want my brother back," he shouted as he charged forward. The goblin stayed still, a huge grin on his face. As Rick got closer the goblin raised his right hand and shot an intense burst of blue light at Rick. Rick went flying through the air and crashed to the floor. He was knocked out. Josie and Amelia ran over to Rick to help him, but he was not responding. The goblin continued to laugh.

"You will have to do better than that," he cackled. Andy started to walk towards the goblin he wanted to get closer to show him that he was not afraid. As he walked forward towards the goblin, the goblin again raised his right hand. Andy thought to himself that this was going to hurt.

The goblin shot out the intense blue light, it struck Andy straight in his chest. Yet he did not go flying back like Rick did. His body glowed bright blue, and he appeared to absorb the energy fired from the goblin.

"You are the chosen one," yelled Billy. The goblin stopped laughing his spell had failed to hurt Andy. Andy now glowing blue could feel this huge amount of energy flowing through his body. He could feel intense power in the tips of his fingers. He fired back the blue light directly to the goblin who deflected it with the book.

"Interesting," said the goblin. "I am The Dark Goblin and you cannot defeat me." Andy smiled.

"I know who you are," he then fired more blue light towards The Dark Goblin who easily deflected this.

The Dark Goblin started to grin.

"Absorb this," he cackled. He placed the book in his bag and raised both hands creating a mini-tornado. He shot this towards Andy. Andy tried to deflect it, but he couldn't. The intense wind sent everyone crashing up against the walls. Andy was now angry and fired a huge intense beam of blue light at The Dark Goblin who was too busy laughing to notice. The blue light hit The Dark Goblin causing him to become dazed. The Goblin grabbed The Spellmaster's book.

"This is not over," he cackled and poof in a puff of smoke he and all the goblins vanished. Andy ran over to the smoke and was kicking the water.

"He got away," screamed Andy.

"Never mind Andy, we have to get Rick out of here." As everyone gathered around Rick, he started to open his eyes.

"Did we win?" he asked. Josie giggled.

"No, he escaped." Rick climbed to his feet, he was soaked through and not amused that he was soaked by sewer water.

"Wow you really stink," joked Josie to Rick. An

unimpressed Rick did not respond he felt embarrassed. He had been beaten so easily by a goblin, yet Andy was still standing.

"I think we should leave and regroup," asked Billy.

"I agree," said Amelia.

"Yeah, I need a shower and I want to get dry," said Rick. A reluctant Andy agreed. He knew he was not ready to defeat The Dark Goblin. He wanted to know about these powers that he had and how he could absorb all that magical energy. As they headed down the passageway and out of the sewer everyone was asking Andy, how he did what he did to The Dark Goblin.

"I do not know what happened, but I am going to find out," said Andy. He felt so confident and believed that he was now the chosen one. On the way through the dockyard Andy would test the powers of the blue light. He would knock over old objects with it. He realised that it was not as powerful as The Dark Goblins, and he would have to find a way to channel and develop his newly learned abilities. As they climbed through the gap in the fence and headed to the main road, Billy was not paying attention. He stepped into the road and everyone gasped as a truck was moving too fast. Andy raised his hand and shouted.

"No!"

The bus just stopped instantly. Undamaged and within a very shaken Billy, stood only a few inches away from the bonnet.

"How did you do that?" asked Josie. "I don't know," replied Andy.

"You not only can absorb high amounts of energy; you also have telekinesis," muttered Amelia.

"What is that?" asked Rick.

"It is where you can move objects using only your mind," replied Amelia. Andy looked at his hands, had he really just stopped that thirty-tonne truck with just his mind? Had The Dark Goblin unleashed his true abilities, when he hit Andy with that high energy blast? Andy tried to think back to a point in his life when something like this had happened before, but nothing would come to him. Then Josie spoke out.

"Andy do you remember when we were younger, and the dog knocked the bookshelf over. I was stood underneath the book shelf yet the bookshelf did not fall on me, it strangely fell to the side. We both thought this was impossible at the time. But now after today I don't think so." Andy started to think back to his memories, he knew Josie was right.

"I have had this in me all this time," he said to the others. A still stunned Billy was now being comforted by Amelia.

"We need to get him home," she said.

"Yeah I got to bounce," said Rick as he ran across the road. Josie and Amelia both linked arms with Billy and walked him home. Andy and Josie then headed home after and entered through the backdoor where their mum was waiting for them.

"Where have you both been and why on earth do you smell like sewage?" Andy and Josie looked at each other, they quickly needed to find an excuse, one that was believable.

"Oh, we were at the park and one of the sprinklers set off, the smell was disgusting Mum," said Josie. Andy nodded in agreement.

"Go and get changed and both of you, please take a shower." Feeling relieved Andy and Josie ran upstairs. Josie got to the bathroom first and locked the door. Andy didn't care he headed to his bedroom and loaded up his computer.

He started to search the internet for energy-based magic. He came across some myths from ancient Greek gods. But he could not find anything about The Spellmaster's Book and the blue light energy. He was beginning to become frustrated until he found something.

"The blue energy blast is used to stun and put others to sleep."

This explains why Rick was knocked out so easily. Andy then found something, it appeared that The Dark Goblin may have many other surprises up his sleeve. He found the tornado used to force people back. But the list was endless. Andy started to write them all down, he wanted to learn about all the magic that could be used against him and how he could set up a defence to counter the spells set upon him and his friends from The Dark Goblin.

10

JOSIE SOON CAME OUT OF THE BATHROOM.

"Hey stinky. You can have a shower now," she said to Andy. Andy was not listening he was too focused on doing his research into some of the spells that could be used on him. He learned that anyone who could absorb blue energy light could use this same energy back, however, there was a limit. Once all the energy had been used, he would have to find a way to absorb more. "Hey, do you think I will be able to create my own spells?" Andy said to Josie. "I hope so, because it would be really lame if you had to keep getting hit by that from that ugly slime ball," replied Josie.

Andy started to search for dark magic on his computer. He also texted Billy, to see if Amelia knew of any where he could find ways to learn about his new-found abilities. It did not take long before his phone started to ring, it was Amelia.

"Hey Andy, so I have been doing some research and the blue light is known as an energy blast. It is very common with magi's but not so common from a spell book, also the tornado is a spell. It's known as the whirling vortex." Andy listened to Amelia and then stopped her.

"I have read up on this. What I need to know is there a way I can make the energy myself without having to absorb it every time?" Amelia paused; Andy could hear her flicking through the pages of her book.

"Andy, you managed to hold that truck back and stop it. According to the book you have this power already you just need to channel it through your mind." Andy started to focus on a pen on his desk. He stared at it deeply and tried to move it. Nothing happened.

"It's not working," he said in frustration down the phone as he said that all his wardrobe doors flew open.

"What was that?" asked Amelia down the phone.

"Oh, I think I know what to do." Andy then hung up and turned to Josie, who had started to close all the wardrobe doors.

"I have to channel my emotions, when I get angry it just happens."

"Yes, I think you are right," replied Josie. Andy then focused back on the pen on the desk he thought of things that made him angry. The pen did not move again.

"Channel them," whispered Josie. Andy closed his eyes and took himself to his own happy place. An old treehouse dad had built for him when he was younger. This was his den, his secret hideout a place that he would always feel safe. Suddenly the pen started to lift off the table. Andy opened his eyes and saw the pen elevated above the desk. He then held his hands open palm to palm. Closed his eyes and blue light started to emit from his hands absorbing back into the other hand.

"I did it, I must be the chosen one." Josie was amazed her brother was magical, and he did not need The Spellmaster's Book to be magical either.

"Well, Dark Goblin you have finally met your match," laughed Andy. Josie started to giggle.

"I wouldn't go that far yet."

"Josie, take a video on my phone so I can send it to Billy. He won't believe this." Josie picked up Andy's phone and begun to make a short video clip.

"Here you go." Andy grabbed the phone and quickly sent the video off to Billy.

The reply was almost instant, it said "that is so cool." Andy felt invincible. His new found powers were going to make him the ultimate weapon, the breaker of the curse.

"I need a superhero name," joked Andy. Josie burst out in laughter.

"That is the funniest thing I have heard all day." Andy then started to laugh with Josie.

"I take it this means we are going back into the sewers?" asked Josie.

"Of course, we are," replied Andy. Andy sat back down at his computer and started to research more about his own abilities, he wanted to unleash his full potential. He wanted to be the one who would dethrone The Dark Goblin and claim The Spellmaster's book. As he was flicking through search engine he came across some old stories. They were talking about a woman from long ago, who had the ability to move anything with her mind. She was so powerful that she could defeat entire armies solo. He continued to read the legend. It spoke of other mythical beings like The Dark Goblin who had even more power. This woman defeated the giant sea serpent and with the aid of three others was able to conquer the mountains and slay one of the leaders of all the monsters. Andy was so interested in this story that he could just not stop reading. There were five other leaders who the mythical beings worshipped. They were so powerful that the four heroes fell before them and were enslaved in a glass box for all of eternity.

Andy then clicked onto the next page where he could see a few of the mythical beings, that worshipped these god-like monsters. As he flicked through them, he gasped, there he was The Dark Goblin.

"So, The Dark Goblin is not the ultimate power then," he said loudly. Andy's door swung open and Josie came running into the room.

"What do you mean he is not the ultimate power?"

"Look," replied Andy. Josie started to read the information off Andy's computer. Shocked and stunned she dropped her drink on the floor.

"My carpet," wailed Andy.

"Never mind the carpet, if The Dark Goblin is as powerful as we know he is then how powerful are these celestials," asked Josie.

"I don't know, but right now they are not important," replied Andy. "We need to focus on the goblins first. Once we have The Spellmaster's Book we will have leverage. Josie not wanting to sound condescending, couldn't hold it in.

"If The Spellmaster's Book is that powerful then why hasn't The Dark Goblin already used it to become a celestial?" Andy then looked straight at Josie, a concerned look over his face his response was simple.

"We are not fighting the celestials."

Josie went back to her room and headed to bed, it was very late, Andy was tired. He climbed into bed and turned off his light. He started to drift off until he heard the bins fall over in the back yard. He jumped out of bed and looked out of his window. He could see the bins had been knocked over and there was garbage all over the grass. Thinking nothing of it, Andy climbed back into bed and tried to go to sleep. Again, there was another bang in the garden. Andy headed downstairs this time to see what was going on. He slowly opened the back door and headed into the garden. One of the metal bins rolled past him.

"Who's there?" shouted Andy. There was no response, it was silent other than a slight whistle in the wind. Andy thought to himself that maybe it was just a gust of wind. He turned to head back into the house until something hit him in the back. Andy stopped and bent down it was a banana skin. Andy quickly turned around to see who had thrown this, but there was no one there.

"Who's there?" shouted Andy again. Suddenly two eyes lit up in the bushes in the corner of the garden.

"Show yourself, I am not afraid," called Andy. The bushes started to rustle and out of the shadows stepped a goblin. The goblin did not charge at Andy. It just stood on the grass at the end of the garden. Not sure on what to do, Andy sent a burst of blue energy in the direction of the goblin. The energy hit the goblin and knocked it to the floor. Andy ran over to the goblin to see if it was harmed. The goblin just lay on the floor with its eyes open.

"Who are you?" shouted Andy to the goblin. The goblin turned his eyes to Andy.

"Help us." Andy jumped up to his feet, the sound of the goblin asking for help sent shivers down his spine.

"Who are you?" Andy demanded again.

"I am your dad," replied the goblin. Andy could feel his knees going weak. How had his father managed to keep his memories? Andy knelt back down to the goblin and placed his arms on the goblin's shoulder.

"Dad you're ok, I will break this curse and I will free you."

As Andy said his words the garden erupted into a thick intense cloud of smoke. Andy climbed back to his feet and looked at the smoke. The goblin that had been lying on the floor then started to cackle. It was a trap, as the smoke cleared The Dark Goblin was there standing tall an axe in one hand and The Spellmaster's book in another.

"We meet again chosen one," sniggered The Dark Goblin. Andy started fire blasts of blue energy straight at The Dark Goblin, who just laughed as he deflected every shot Andy could fire. The Dark Goblin then started to taunt Andy.

"Hit me if you can." Andy was now becoming frustrated his powers were proving to be so infective against The Dark Goblin. Andy could feel his rage flowing through his veins then suddenly he sent such a shockwave that The Dark Goblin was lifted through the air and slammed onto the floor.

"Mmmmm," said The Dark Goblin as he climbed himself back to his feet.

"You are more powerful than I had realised," The Dark Goblin said in a slightly concerned voice. Andy knew that this was his opening. His opportunity to try and defeat The Dark Goblin once and for all.

Andy started to charge up his blue energy with both his hands as he went to blast forward the Dark Goblin hit Andy with dark magic. Andy was frozen in place, and he couldn't move. The Dark Goblin then cackled as he vanished in a thick smog of smoke.

11

THE DARK GOBLIN WAS GONE, THE SMOKE settled. Andy started to feel sensations through his body. He was now able to move. Josie came running into the back garden.

"What was all that noise about?" she asked. A defeated Andy was not really up for much of a conversation.

"It was The Dark Goblin," he replied.

"Well what happened?" Andy ignored Josie and made his way back into the house. How had The Dark Goblin frozen him in the way that he did? What was this form of dark magic used against him? It was almost as like time had stopped which allowed The Dark Goblin to escape. There was a plus side though, he remembered what The Dark Goblin had said to him, about being more powerful than he thought. Andy knew this meant that The Dark Goblin had underestimated him. Andy also knew that he could hurt The Dark Goblin. Not all hope was lost in Andy's mind. He felt defeated, but he needed to know about this powerful spell which could cause him to freeze and how he could counter this using his own powers.

It was far too early for him to call Billy, so he would have to wait until they were all together at school in the morning.

Andy climbed into bed; he could not stop thinking about what had happened. How he was tricked and how The Dark Goblin knew where he lived. The fact that they mentioned his dad really did mess with his mind. Yet it gave Andy hope that one of the goblins was indeed his dad, because if he wasn't there was no way they could know any of the information that he had learned that night. Eventually, Andy closed his eyes and fell into a deep sleep.

The sound of his alarm had woken him, and he headed downstairs.

"Perhaps last night was just a dream," he thought to himself. He went into the back garden to check the bins .There was his mum picking up the rubbish that had been strewn across the garden.

"These raccoons are a nightmare; I am fed-up of cleaning up after these trash panda's," scowled his mum. Andy looked at the state of the garden, last night was not a dream it was reality. The Dark Goblin now knew where he lived. Andy ran back inside and found Josie brushing her hair ready for school.

"Josie do you remember last night?"

"Well, I remember the noise in the garden and coming outside to you looking upset and shaken. What really did happen last night?" she asked.

"He knows where we live, he will be back and I think he can stop time as well. Yet I know I can defeat him, I hurt him. He also said he did not realise how powerful I was," replied Andy.

Josie put down her hairbrush and put her hair in a ponytail.

"This needs to end as soon as possible. If he comes back there is no telling what he would do if he catches us unaware," replied Josie. Andy grabbed his rucksack.

"Let's get to school we need to tell the others. They could also be in danger." Josie grabbed her bag, and they both ran out of the house. They ran to the bus stop but the bus was nowhere in sight.

"Let's run to school, it will be faster than if we wait for this bus all day." Andy then started to run down the road.

"Wait up," called Josie as she gave chase.

As they arrived at the school, they could see Billy and Amelia chatting by the entrance. They ran up to them both out of breath they struggled to get their words out.

"What is going on?" asked Billy. Huffing and puffing and trying to catch their breath Amelia asked if they had run all the way to school.

"Yes" gasped Andy. "We ran all the way here; we have something to tell you."

"Really, spit it out then." Rick had just come around the corner and saw them all chatting. Andy started to catch his breath.

"The Dark Goblin appeared in my garden last night. He knows where I live, he may know where you all live. We had a fight, and he froze me still, before he escaped." Rick started to laugh.

"What are you talking about? Those things only live in the sewers." Billy and Amelia did not find it funny at all they were concerned.

"I thought that it was just the sewers too, but it appears he can teleport as well. He also knew personal things, one of the goblins pretended to be our dad." Andy explained.

Suddenly the bell rang for the start of school there was no more time for Andy to chat about what had happened the previous night.

"We will catch up later," said Billy. Everyone then went to their classes. Andy still in a state of shock from last night wandered into the toilets where he started to splash his face with water. He was so hot and sweaty from the long run to school that he needed to cool down. As he lifted his head to look in the mirror he jumped back. It was not his reflection. It was a reflection of The Dark Goblin stood grinning at him.

"I am watching you," cackled the Goblin as the reflection turned back to Andy's Andy splashed his face again with more cold water and looked up. He could just see himself now looking bright red and hot and sweaty. "What is going on?" he said out loud. The door to the toilets then suddenly flew open.

"Don't you have a class to get to Andy," scowled the principal.

"Yes ma'am."

"Well get to it then," she replied. Andy grabbed his bag and ran out of the toilets. How could The Dark Goblin see him through mirrors what was this new magic? It seemed every time that they both met The Dark Goblin would show off new even more powerful spells or magic. Andy knew that he needed to find ways, other ways to learn how to combat his own abilities. He knew if he was to defeat The Dark Goblin, he would have to start playing dirty.

Andy started walking to class, as he walked past the lockers, he would force some of them to open with his mind. He was starting to fully understand his telekinesis now and how to use it effectively. After he had opened many of the lockers, he turned his attention to some of the lockers the popular kids have. This time he did not open the lockers, he closed his eyes and clenched his fists. He remembered all the horrible things that they had said and done to him, Josie and his friends. With all his might the lockers started to crush down. Not only now could he move things with his mind, he could also cause them damage. The lockers started to fold like an accordion the sound of crushing metal echoing down the halls. The sound of footsteps made Andy open his eyes, he then ran off to his class. He did not stop or think, he forced open the classroom door.

"Good of you to join us Andy," said the English teacher in a very sarcastic tone. Andy did not reply he walked straight over to his desk and slumped down in his chair.

He was now very worried about the mess he had caused in the hallways. He did not want everyone to know about his abilities, that would only give further advantage to The Dark Goblin. As the lesson went on an anxious Andy was biting down on his nails. The vision of The Dark Goblin in the toilets, and the carnage he had caused in the hallway playing on his mind. He could not focus in class, but he didn't care every now and again he would look around him. Amelia was sat in the back of the class, but she did not notice Andy looking over. She was far too engrossed in her classwork. Amelia cared so much for her grades, she wanted to be a scientist her dream to study the mythical being's up close and personal.

The bell went to signal the end of the lesson, Andy grabbed his books and stood up. He waited for Amelia to walk past, as she got close, he started to whisper her name.

"What's up?" she asked.

"I may have destroyed half the lockers in the school."

"Seriously how?" replied Amelia.

"My powers, I saw him in the mirror. It was him, he told me was watching me." Amelia looked concerned; she was worried about Andy as he was clearly not acting himself.

"Let's go and take a look then," replied Amelia. They both walked out of class and down into the hallway. It was clear, all the lockers were perfectly intact.

"This cannot be happening, I destroyed them. I crushed them," cried Andy.

"You should go home and get some rest, Andy. You're exhausted you are not sleeping."

"Hey guys, what's happening?" said Billy as he strolled up the hallway.

"Billy do you see it, do you see all the damaged lockers," Andy said frantically.

"No, everything is all good. Are you ok bro?" replied Billy.

"I was just saying that Andy needed to go home and get some rest," whispered Amelia to Billy. Andy was so frustrated and angry; he knew what had happened, and he heard Amelia whispering to Billy.

"Why do you not believe me?" he screamed. As Andy screamed out the sound of twisting metal could be heard. Everyone in the hallway stopped and stared as the lockers all started to fold in on themselves.

"Andy stop," shouted Josie as she came running over. All the other school kids started to scream.

There was mayhem in the corridors as everyone ran for the exits. Teachers came out of their classrooms as the noise was so intense. Only to see lockers folding and being thrown around the hallways by a mysterious force. But this was no mysterious force this was a very upset Andy.

"Andy it's me Josie, your sister," as she grabbed him by the shoulders. Andy's eyes were now pure white there were no pupils. Wind started to pick up in the hallway and Billy and Amelia started to fear for their lives. They ran and hid behind a bin as Josie was stood in front of Andy trying to help him snap out of his trance. Suddenly there was a loud thud, Andy was knocked to the floor from behind. There was Rick.

"I never thought I would be so glad to see you do that to him," said a very grateful Josie.

"I had no choice; he could have killed someone," said a very upset Rick. "I may have been mean to you guys, but I never actually wanted to hurt anyone like this. But I had to, I am sure you can understand." Billy and Amelia came out of their hiding spot.

"Yeah, totally understand," said Billy. Amelia smiled at Rick and thanked him for his support.

"Best get him home, there is going to be a lot of questions asked about the mess here," said Josie.

Rick and Billy lifted Andy to his feet, Andy was very dazed and started to mutter.

"What happened?" Rick and Billy started to get Andy to move on his feet before Josie simply told Andy that they would talk about this later after he had some rest. A dazed Andy started to have visions; The Dark Goblin was stood directly in front of him.

"You destroyed the school and I cleaned it back up," he said in an aggressive manner. In Andy's mind he asked the goblin why he would do that.

The goblin replied, "displaying powers, will lead to others knowing about us. We will all be hunted down and destroyed." Andy then opened his eyes properly and could see that he was laying on his bed with a cold compress on his head.

He was so confused, why would The Dark Goblin not want the world to know about magic, about spells or the endless amounts of power they had. Nothing made sense apart from when he said about people hunting them down. Were there bounty hunters out there, people who hunted the mythical monsters for trophies, or were the other powerful beings wanting to bring peace to the world. The ideas were endless, and they would not just leave Andy's mind.

THE FOLLOWING DAY ANDY WOKE UP, HE HAD A
massive headache and huge lump on the back of his
head, from where Rick had hit him. Josie was sat at
the bottom of his bed.

"How are you feeling today?" Andy sat up.

"I feel like I have taken a huge hit to the back of
my head". Josie sniggered.

"Yeah that was Rick."

"Well why?" replied Andy.

"Do you not remember?" she asked.

"Remember what?" replied Andy. Josie let out a
really long sigh.

"Yesterday at school, what you did was really
terrifying. You crushed lockers and threw them
around like they were softballs. You scared everyone

out of the school, even the teachers. You even scared Billy and Amelia half to death. You really scared me, your eyes were just pure white, you looked possessed by some kind of demon." Andy's jaw just hung open in shock. He did not remember any of that, nothing at all. All he could remember was the visions, in his dreams of the conversations that he had with The Dark Goblin. The rest he had no memory of at all and that scared him.

"We need to go back; I have to face him. This time to the end." Josie stood up off Andy's bed.

"Yes, we do, but you need to learn to control your temper before you accidentally kill someone." Andy did not want to bring harm to anyone. He wanted to help people, to save them not be the one who has caused them harm and misery. Andy slipped out of his bed and checked his phone. He had a message from Billy. He unlocked his phone and read the message.

"Hope you are feeling better today bro."

Andy smiled, he may have scared Billy half to death, but at least he still cared about him.

"I will learn to control my anger, but this time no ice cubes. I am going to get us some carbon dioxide, fire extinguishers," said Andy.

"Basically, dry ice, what an excellent idea," replied

Josie. "But where do you think you can get them from?" Andy just smiled.

"Rick."

Josie headed out of Andy's room, so he could get ready. He jumped onto his computer and sent Rick a message through social media. Asking him to get four carbon dioxide, fire extinguishers, one each for Josie, Billy, Amelia, and Rick. Andy did not need one, his mind was his weapon. He knew where he could find The Dark Goblin. Andy had decided that he was not going to let them come to him. But instead, he was going to bring the fight, down in the sewers in The Dark Goblins home.

"Can I come in?" said a voice at the door. It was his mum.

"Sure, mum are you ok?" asked Andy.

"No, not at all. I was wondering if you had heard from your dad at all. The police have said, they have found nothing in the sewers, there was not even a trace that they had been working in there."

Andy not wanting to alarm his mum or make her aware of the goblins said, "no, but I do miss him." Andy's mum gave him a kiss on the head.

"Do not ride your bike in the dark, next time you may not be so lucky." She then left the room. Andy then turned his attention back to his social media. He was hoping to see if there was anything posted about what had happened in school the previous day. But there was nothing, it was like everyone's memory had been wiped. People were posting as normal.

"Josie come here?" shouted Andy out of his bedroom door. Josie came into Andy's room.

"Has anyone mentioned anything to you about what happened yesterday at school?" Josie started to look very confused.

"Well, what did happen at school yesterday? Seemed like a pretty normal day to me?" A dumbfounded Andy then realised that everyone's memory had been wiped about that day, but how? He did not do anything, yet he could remember the conversation Josie had with him earlier. It then clicked; The Spellmaster's Book has a spell in it that can clear the minds of anyone, but only for the last 24 hours.

"He must have cast a spell on everyone, no one remembers. Come on Josie we have to get to school and fast." Andy grabbed his things and didn't even stop to brush his teeth. He ran out of the door and caught the early bus with Josie.

As they arrived at school everyone was acting perfectly normal, and they were all going about their business.

"Hey guys," said Billy who was waiting with Amelia in their usual spot. Andy did not take notice today and ran straight into the school to see if there was any damage. Again, the school was fine, nothing out of place. The Dark Goblin clearly did not want many people to know about himself. Perhaps he was just trying to protect The Spellmaster's Book, or maybe just himself. Andy then walked back outside to catch up with the others.

"Do any of you remember what happened yesterday?" asked Andy.

"Yeah, we came to school had some lessons, ate some lunch and then went home?" laughed Billy. Andy knew no one had a clue about what had happened. Not until Rick arrived shortly after.

"I remember?" he said. Andy felt a sigh of relief he wasn't going crazy after all. Rick then grabbed Andy and put him in a headlock rubbing his knuckles on the top of his head.

"Yeah I remember I was going to do this?" Rick laughed as he let go.

"What you do that for?" said Andy as he rubbed his head to try and remove the burning sensation.

"No reason, because I want to. Anyway, why do you want those fire extinguishers?" said Rick.

"Why do you think? you big dummy," laughed Amelia.

"Oh yeah, they are cold! and don't you call me a dummy." He then raised his fist towards Amelia and pushed past her as he walked into school.

"That was totally unnecessary," moaned Amelia.

"He really did not need to raise his fist to me like that." Amelia then turned to Billy.

"Why did you not step in and defend me?" Billy dropped his head down in shame.

"I'm sorry," he replied.

"Don't worry Billy, Andy used to be terrified of him as well it's nothing to worry about," said Josie jumping to Billy's defence. Amelia just rolled her eyes.

"I am going in anyone coming?" she asked. Everyone then started to follow Amelia into school. A very embarrassed Billy whispered "thank you" to Josie as they headed inside.

At lunch, Rick arrived at the table where everyone was having lunch.

"I have them," he whispered. He then walked out of the cafeteria.

"What does he have?" asked Billy.

"Carbon dioxide fire extinguishers," replied Andy.

"What a brilliant idea, but won't they be useless against The Dark Goblin?" asked Amelia.

"Yes, they will, but you guys need some protection against the rest of the goblins. Otherwise, we will just be overrun before we could even get close to The Dark Goblin."

"So, when do we do this?" asked Josie.

"We go first light on Saturday morning. This time we will not leave until we prevail." The bell rang for the end of lunch. Everyone grabbed their things and headed off to the final few hours of school. Saturday was only two days away, and they now had a battle plan, one that could actually work this time.

13

Saturday morning appeared to arrive very quickly, almost out of nowhere. Andy and Josie had not slept much the previous night as there was so much going on in their minds. Today was the final day, the last attempt. Andy was calling it the final battle as this was it to him. It was win or lose there was no quit, not anymore. He packed his things, a torch, the map, and a drink if he was to become thirsty. He did not need his catapult. His abilities now were in tune, and he knew how to control them much better than when he faced The Dark Goblin on their last encounter.

Josie came bursting into Andy's room, she was dressed in bright colours this time and not all in back. Her logic was to be bright so the others could see her.

"You go from one extreme to the next Josie," laughed Andy.

"Yeah, yeah you can laugh but you will see this will be beneficial to the team," she joked back.

"You ready?"

"Yeah as ready as I'll ever be." They both picked up their bags and headed downstairs. As they got to the bottom of the stairs, they could hear their mum crying in the living room.

"Let's go and see her?" said Josie. Andy could not bear to see his mum struggling as she was, she missed their dad so much perhaps even more than both Andy and Josie.

They opened the door to the lounge; there she was their mum face buried into a cushion sobbing uncontrollably. Both Andy and Josie sat down each side of their mum and took a hand each. They cuddled into her before Andy whispered.

"We will find dad and we will bring him back." Their mum continued to cry. It was so upsetting for both Andy and Josie to see.

"We need to get moving," said Andy. Josie nodded and Andy and Josie left their mum still sat on the sofa. They headed out of the house and made their way to the new meeting point at the fence outside the old dockyard.

There was nobody there when they arrived, it was quiet.

"I told them to be here," said Andy. He was so impatient and was starting to become grumpy after a few minutes Rick showed up. He had with him the four fire extinguishers as requested.

"Have you seen Billy and Amelia?" asked Andy.

"No," replied Rick. After another short wait, they both appeared from around the corner walking hand in hand and giggling to one another.

"What time do you call this?" snapped Andy.

"Hey, we are here to help you, no need to be like that?" snapped Billy back.

"Ok boys calm down, we have a mission to complete, let's not start a war with one another," pleaded Josie.

"Ok, Billy, I am sorry."

"No hard feelings bro."

"You lot ready or are you going to kiss and make up?" laughed Rick.

"No, we are ready," replied Andy. The gap in the fence was still there, thankfully to everyone they did not have to lift it out its support anymore. They all squeezed through and made their way down to the large entrance to the sewer. Rick started to hand out the fire extinguishers.

"Only use these if you have to, do not fire them at each other," his instructions were simple, and everyone was confident that they knew what they had to do. They connected their torches to their heads using their new straps they had bought and slowly started to walk into the sewer.

The smell was even stronger, the smell of rotting flesh.

"This is so disgusting," moaned Josie. She whipped out a face mask she had been carrying and put it over her nose and mouth.

"Biohazard eh?" joked Amelia. Josie took no notice as they continued walking into the sewer, the light from the torches would reflect the steam coming off the shallow water that was underneath their feet. It did not take long before they arrived, at the slimy remains of the goblin that Andy had melted with his catapult.

"I guess this explains the foul smell?" said Andy.

"Yeah, I agree," replied Rick.

"Come on let's keep moving they are down here somewhere." They all continued forward, further down the passageway and deeper into the dark sewers. It was silent this time, there was no sound other than their footsteps through the water. There was not even a sound of a single rat.

Something was different this time, it was soooooo quiet.

"It feels like we are in some kind of horror film doesn't it?" said Josie. Everyone stopped and looked at Josie.

"This is a horror film," replied Billy. As they moved forwards, they arrived at the wall with the small gap in it. Andy peered through and the room was full of goblins. This time they were asleep.

"I think we have a golden opportunity here guys," he whispered.

"Why, what is it?"

"They are all asleep, we can avoid them and find The Dark Goblin." As they made their way around the room, they found an entrance to the large rooms where all the goblins were asleep.

"He has to be in that room?" said Andy.

"So, we are going in then?" asked Josie. Andy started to open the small wooden door that led into the room. There was a slight creak and some of the goblins started to stir.

"Sssshhhh, don't wake them," whispered Josie. Andy managed to open the door and stepped into the room. He could see all the goblins laying on the floor in front of him, but yet there was no sign of The Dark Goblin himself.

"Where could he be?" moaned Andy.

"There," said Josie, she had spotted a double door with gold handles.

"Another room," said Andy, he carefully made his way around the sleeping goblins on the floor and reached the large wooden door. He placed his hand on the door handle and turned the knob. The door slowly opened.

"I have been expecting you," cackled The Dark Goblin, he was sat at a desk in the corner of his room with The Spellmaster's Book open. He was clearly reading this.

"This ends now," shouted Andy to The Dark Goblin.

The Dark Goblin stood up, he let out an almighty roar awakening all the sleeping goblins in the room behind. Without thinking, Rick ran into The Dark Goblins room. He snatched The Spellmaster's Book from his desk.

"Rick, no," shouted Andy. But it was too late, Rick was now part of the curse. He dropped to the floor and started to scream in pain, his body started to contort in all shapes. His skin changing to green, then it was silent, he turned around and there was Rick, a goblin. He had now been cursed like the others.

"See you will not defeat me, you and your friends will all become my servants." Andy turned around he could see Billy, Josie, and Amelia all with their backs together armed with their fire extinguishers waiting for the goblins to pounce. Andy was in two minds; did he help his friends, or did he take on The Dark Goblin and try to end this once and for all.

ANDY FIRED AN ENERGY BLAST INTO THE LARGE room stunning many goblins, he had bought his friends some time. He then turned to The Dark Goblin who was smiling at him. Andy fired his blue energy at The Dark Goblin who just absorbed this into his chest.

"You need to do better than that," he sniggered. Andy then braced himself. The Dark Goblin sent a huge shockwave through the floor that launched Andy into the air. The shockwave was that powerful, that it knocked the other goblins down in the room behind. Andy stayed down on the floor; he was now going to play dirty. He waited for The Dark Goblin to come towards him, the trick worked. The Dark Goblin made his way towards Andy giggling and laughing, as he got close Andy used his telekinetic abilities. He threw The Dark Goblin onto the ceiling then back down on the floor.

"You little…" shouted The Dark Goblin.

Whilst he was down on the floor Andy turned his attention to his friends who were using the fire extinguisher very effectively. The goblin army started to back off and the fight was turning in the direction of Andy and his friends. Suddenly Andy was attacked from behind. He was knocked to the floor. He shot an energy blast behind him and it blasted the goblin off his back. He turned over to see that it was once Rick, but now a goblin.

"Rick, I do not want to hurt you. If you can hear me, you don't have to do this," said Andy. The goblin stared at Andy and charged. Andy stopped the charging goblin mid charge with his powers.

"Rick please, you do not need to do this!" shouted Andy again. He could see the expression on the goblins face changing. Andy let the goblin go and he stopped. The goblin then turned to The Dark Goblin and charged at him. The Dark Goblin pulled out his axe and swung it as Rick the Goblin charged him. Andy screamed out in horror; The Dark Goblin had severed the head of Rick.

"You will not defeat me for I am eternal," said

The Dark Goblin. He fired a fireball at Andy who managed to dodge this. The Dark Goblin then picked up The Spellmaster's Book, He started to chant a phrase from the book. Behind him opened what looked like a large hole, but this was not just any hole. This was a portal. The Dark Goblin started to laugh and stepped backwards into the portal disappearing. Andy could see the portal closing and ran as fast as he could. He dived forward and straight into the portal.

The Goblins in the room all started to change back into humans.

"Josie," shouted a voice. It was her dad; he was free from the curse.

"Where is Andy?" Everyone started looking frantically for Andy, he must have broken the curse. But no one could see where he was or what had happened. Josie ran into The Dark Goblins room where she saw Rick on the floor, who was all back together again in one piece.

"Rick where is Andy?" said Josie who was getting frantically concerned for the whereabouts of her brother.

"He went, with him through the hole in the wall," replied Rick.

"Hole in the wall, what are you talking about?"

Amelia and Billy stepped into the room with some of the other people who had been trapped in the spell.

"It is a portal, a powerful magic spell that can take you to any dimension," replied Amelia.

"Well we need to open the portal," wailed Josie.

"It is no use; Andy will have to do that when he claims The Spellmaster's Book," replied Amelia.

"Josie, let's help all these people get out of here?"

Rick had finally regained his focus, squinting his eyes they slowly adjusted. To his amazement there he was, his little brother.

Rick was overjoyed, his little brother who had not aged a single day was sat on the floor. Looking very lost and confused.

"Brother" shouted Rick who ran over to his brother to embrace all the time that they had lost.

"You have grown Rick." Rick started to laugh and smile, he was overjoyed to have his baby brother back.

"Rick come on" shouted Billy. He grabbed his brother by the arm and followed everyone down the long passageways.

When they left the sewers, they had learned that some of the people that had been saved had been goblins for many decades. Only having memories up until the point that they were turned into goblins. When they got into the dockyards Billy called for help on his phone. It did not take long for the police and paramedics to arrive. The police were shocked as some of the people had been missing for almost 80 years, yet they had not aged a single day. None knew what to make of things. Everyone was very confused as to what had happened and how it had happened.

"Let's get you home?" said Josie's dad. Josie did not want to go home, she wanted to go back in there to find Andy and bring him back to safety.

When they both arrived home, their mum was overjoyed with relief that their dad had come home safely.

"Where have you been darling?" she asked.

"It is a very long story; I will tell you another time. But right now, I need a long hot shower." Josie headed upstairs and went into Andy's room. She turned on his computer in hope of finding a way to open up the portal to bring him back to them. She did not want to have to explain to their mum that they had brought back their dad, but in return had lost Andy to another realm somewhere in the universe. All she could find on the computer was that the spell could only be made from using The Spellmaster's Book. There had to be another way surely.

Andy fell from what seemed like a great height

landing on a beach near a shoreline. What was this place and why was he alone? The Dark Goblin could be heard cackling in the distance but was nowhere to be seen. Andy started to make his way down the beach, not a person in sight. He turned and looked at the ocean before him, calm and relaxed with the sun beating down on it. On the other side was dense trees, it looked like a jungle. A huge roar erupted in the air Andy froze in shock. This was not the roar of The Dark Goblin, but the roar of something else. Something much bigger much bigger. He looked up into the sky and could see a large bird with flames all over its wings. What was going on?

"I told you that you couldn't win. You're in Mytherios now," laughed The Dark Goblin, who then disappeared in a puff of black smoke. Andy continued to look around. The large bird had vanished, but then something else caught his attention. Something in the water, this enormous tentacle popped out of the water and tried to pull Andy into the sea. He jumped over it and started to run into the jungle where he could hear the sounds of the leaves rustling all around him.

"What is this place?" said Andy to himself. He had no idea now if he was being hunted. This time he was alone in this world, a world of monsters. He not only had The Dark Goblin to contend with, but a world of large beasts. Andy continued to make his way through the deep thick forest. Eventually, he came to a clearing and there was a woman with her back to him. She had long red hair and was holding something yellow in her hand.

"You do not belong here?" said the woman.

"I know I don't, what is this place?" asked Andy. The woman turned around and Andy was so stunned to see such a beautiful woman, before him. She then opened out these large white wings.

"You are a fairy?" asked Andy.

"You need to leave now," replied the woman. Andy did not want to leave; everything was so frightening to him here.

Suddenly he was back the beach.

"What the?" he said to himself extremely confused and dazed.

"Why am I back here?" he replied. The ground then started to shake heavily and in the distance, Andy could see that one of the mountains started to wobble. Something powerful was in that mountain, something massive and very angry. Scared and afraid he called out to The Dark Goblin.

"What is this place Dark Goblin." The Dark Goblin appeared behind Andy.

"You are in a whole new world. Find the four who

are entombed, and you may find your way back home." In another puff of smoke, The Dark Goblin had vanished.

"The Four…" Andy said out loud. Then it clicked the four that were trapped. He looked forward at the mountain which was still shaking violently. He knew he could no longer be afraid. He took a deep breath and stepped off the beach back into the trees, ready to find the four.

THE END

If you enjoyed *The Spellmaster's Book*, please check out *Pherra Rises*, Book Two in the Legends of Mytherios.

See more at www.JamesKeith.co.uk

ABOUT THE AUTHOR

James Keith is a knowledgeable professional with almost 20 years of proficiency in the healthcare industry. James has always been an activist for mental health due to his own experiences in the field.

James wants people to be aware of how to deal with emotional, psychological, and social well-being issues and how to stop them from affecting their lives.

Follow James at
www.JamesKeith.co.uk

facebook.com/jameskeith86

twitter.com/JamesKeith86

instagram.com/jamesikeith